I would like to thank my family and friends for their support. My wife Lisa has been my editor and partner. My children: Ava and Marty: your love of reading and of my book makes me smile. My nieces and nephews (Naomi, Sarah, Ellie, Ben, Sam, Maisie, Rachel, Harry, and Julia) are all characters. Thanks also to my parents (Nana and PopPop), in-laws and siblings. Special thanks also to my colleagues (Marlene and Mary C., in particular). Thanks to Jackie for your great illustrations! This book has been ten years in the making!

—Brad/Uncle Brad/Daddy ☺

Thank you to my family and friends. To my parents who encouraged me to draw and took me to the zoo, thank you. To my husband Eliezer, thank you for your critiques and support. Thank you to my children, Ezra and Maya, who love to read and draw and make me smile.

—Jackie / Mommy

ISBN: 1477474129
ISBN-13: 9781477474129
Library of Congress Control Number: 2012908878

CreateSpace Independent Publishing Platform
North Charleston, South Carolina

Nana and the Banana is dedicated to Nana,
also known as Mom, Mrs. B, and Sydnee.

Nana and the Banana

By Brad Burgunder
Illustrated by Jackie Ross

Naomi and her Nana were walking through the Zoo.

They found a banana, but didn't know what to do.
"Who lost this banana?" Naomi asked Nana.

Nana sighed, "Naomi please don't pout. Let's go on an adventure to find out."

So the two – one in red, the other in blue –
started their journey in the Zoo.

First they came upon Sarah the bear,
a big animal, with light brown hair.

"My name is Naomi and this is my Nana.
We wondered if maybe you lost this banana."
Sarah smiled and tapped her feet, "No thanks!
I eat mostly red meat."

So the two – one in red, the other in blue – went searching for a clue.

They strolled into the barn
and met a black horse.

Harry had a long tail
on his back, of course.

"My name is Naomi and this is my Nana. We wondered if maybe you lost this banana." Harry rolled his eyes, grunted, and neighed.

He said, "*Everyone* knows that horses eat hay."
And before Naomi or Nana could think what to say,
Harry galloped away to enjoy the warm day.

As they walked away, they saw the baby elephant Ellie, playing in the dirt and rolling on her belly. "My name is Naomi and this is my Nana. We wondered if maybe you lost this banana."

Ellie said, "I prefer peanuts in the shell, oranges, or anything with a good smell."

So they walked down the path,
until they reached Julia, the giraffe.

Naomi could hardly see the giraffe's ear. She made a face and sighed, "Oh, my dear."

"My name is Naomi and this is my Nana. We wondered if maybe you lost this banana."
The giraffe didn't know where she should go. She shook her neck side to side, "No."

So the two went on
– one in red, the
other in blue – to
another part of
the Zoo.

At the Reptile House, they saw a gray mouse. "Mr. Mouse," asked Naomi, "do boas eat bananas?" A boa named Ben looked up and hissed at Nana.

The mouse let out a squeak
and ran and hid, whispering,
"No Miss, they don't...but I
sure wish they did."

The two – one in blue, the other in red – were at a real dead end.

Rachel, the white rabbit hopped over with some news. "Your answer," she told them, "lies near the front of the zoo."

At the swimming hole, they saw Sammy the seal, eating some fish for his meal.

Sammy flipped a ball into the trees, and woke a hive of buzzing bees.

Nana picked up Naomi and they ran to the manta ray of the seas. Maisie glided through the water with the greatest of ease.

"My name is Naomi and this is my Nana.
We wondered if maybe you lost this banana."
Maisie dove down and swam on by.
The two left her to feed on some plankton pie.

At last they found Ava, the lioness, who was smart and proud. She let out a roar that was really quite loud.

She lived in a cage that was ten feet tall.
Maybe she could solve this mystery once and for all.
"My name is Naomi and this is my Nana. We
wondered if maybe you lost this banana."

Ava roared, "Try that hungry monkey, Marty, hanging from a vine." Naomi grabbed Nana, "Hurry, we don't have much time."

They picked up the pace until they reached the gate.
It was really beginning to get quite late.

"My name is Naomi and this is my Nana.
Could this really be your banana?"

To her surprise, the monkey
screeched and took the banana.

"Thank you ladies," he said to Naomi and her Nana.

THE END!